Published by Scholastic Inc.
90 Old Sherman Turnpike, Danbury, Connecticut 06816.

ISBN 0-7172-8494-8

Designed and produced by Bill SMITH STUDIO.

Printed in the U.S.A.
First printing, September 2002

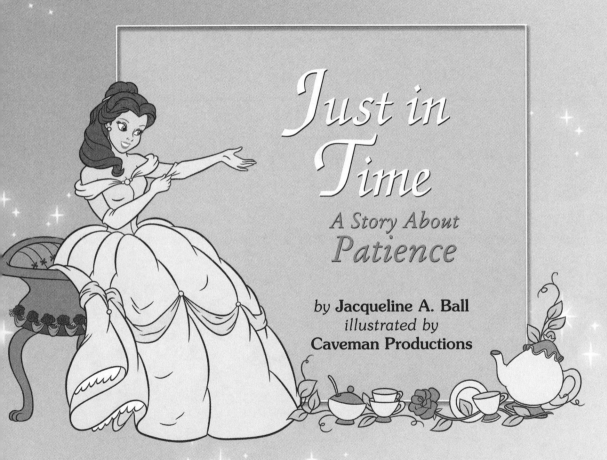

Just in Time

A Story About *Patience*

by **Jacqueline A. Ball**
illustrated by
Caveman Productions

SCHOLASTIC INC.

New York   Toronto   London   Auckland   Sydney
Mexico City   New Delhi   Hong Kong   Buenos Aires

Outside the Beast's castle, snowflakes swirled. But in the kitchen, all was warm and cheerful.

"Are the gingersnaps ready yet?" asked Chip.

"No, dear," answered his mother, Mrs. Potts. "They need time to bake."

Chip frowned. "But I want some now!"

"Now, now," said his mother.
"You must be patient."

"*W*hat does *being patient* mean?" Chip asked. "It means understanding that sometimes you have to wait," Mrs. Potts answered.

"*P*erhaps Belle will go outside and play with you until the gingersnaps are ready," she continued. "We were working on her knitting, but I think she's in the library now."

Chip perked up. "All right."

*I*n the Beast's library, Belle was reading a book. She was at an exciting part when—

"Belle! Belle!" Chip called. He was perched on the arm of her chair.

"Hello, Chip," Belle said, smiling at the little teacup.

"Belle, can you come out to the barn and play hide-and-seek with me? Please? Please, *please?*"

Belle put down her book. "Of course."

"Yippee!" cried Chip.

Snowdrifts blocked the path to the barn.

The Beast was clearing it.

"We'll help you," Belle called.

"But I want to play!" Chip complained.

"After the job is done," she promised.

Working together, Chip, Belle, and the Beast quickly cleared the snow away. The Beast returned to the castle.

"*Now* let's play!" Chip said. "I'll be *it*."

Belle ran and hid behind a tree.

"*F*ound you!" said Chip. "Now you're *it*."

"I have an idea that I want to do first," Belle said. "Let's make bird feeders. The birds look hungry. The snow is covering their food."

"*H*ow do we make a bird feeder?" Chip
wanted to know.

Belle pulled a ball of red wool out of her pocket.
"We can use this. Would you please ask your
mother for some honey while I pick some berries?"

When Chip returned, they dipped pinecones into the honey and stuck berries on them. Then they hung the feeders from a tree. They waited . . . and waited.

"They'll come," said Belle. "You have to be—"
"Patient," finished Chip, sighing. "I know."
And sure enough, birds soon came.

Chip and Belle went back to their game. "One, two, three," Belle counted, "four, five, six, seven . . .

. . . $\mathcal{E}$ighteen, nineteen, twenty. Ready or not, here I come!" Belle called.

Chip squeezed through the open barn door.

What was that noise? It sounded like a horse, except . . . muffled.

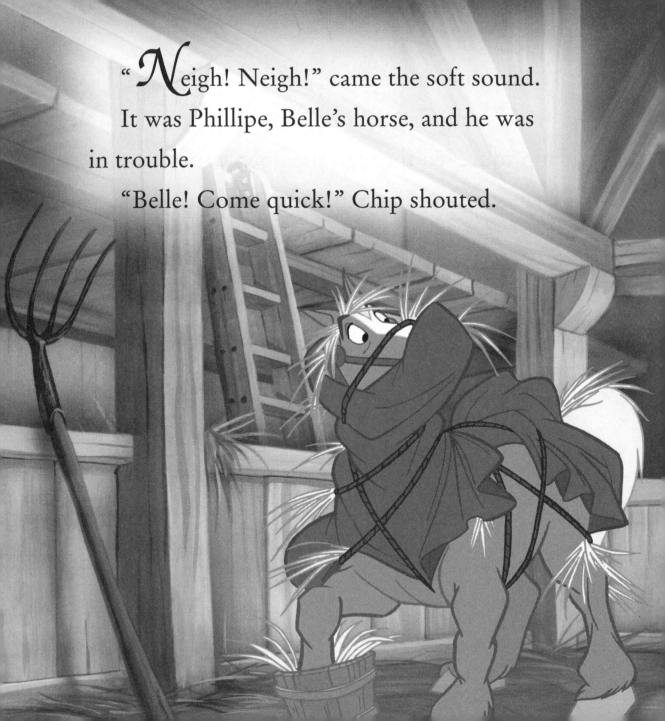

"Neigh! Neigh!" came the soft sound.
It was Phillipe, Belle's horse, and he was
in trouble.

"Belle! Come quick!" Chip shouted.

Belle rushed inside and saw Phillipe all tangled up in a rope and blanket. "Oh, my!" exclaimed Belle. "What happened?"

𝒯hen Belle remembered. "I was supposed to feed him! I forgot all about it! Phillipe got tangled up trying to reach his food. We need to get help!"

"I know what to do!" said Chip.

*H*e hopped to a rope hanging down from a big bell. Chip jumped up and swung on the rope. *Clang! Clang!* rang the bell.

*H*earing the noise, Mrs. Potts came bouncing, spilling tea on her way.

The Beast came dashing out.

Cogsworth the clock huffed and puffed along.

*L*umiere the candlestick came out, melting the snow as he ran.

They all raced into the barn and stared in silence when they saw Phillipe.

"*Mon Dieu!*" exclaimed Lumiere.

"Oh, dear," said Mrs. Potts.

"What a predicament!" agreed Cogsworth.

"What happened?" asked the Beast.

"*P*hillipe wasn't being patient," explained Chip. "Right, Belle?"

"Yes," agreed Belle. "But it isn't his fault. It's mine. I forgot to feed him, and he was hungry."

Then everyone tried to help at once.
Soon they were all arguing about what to do.

"I'll burn through the ropes!" shouted
Lumiere.

"I'll break them apart!" yelled the Beast.

"*I*'ll pour him some tea," suggested
Mrs. Potts. "The poor thing is probably thirsty."

Everyone was in such a hurry. No one was
being patient.

Soon Phillipe was more tangled than before.

*B*elle stepped back and watched the confusion. *What would a princess do?*

"Please!" Belle called. "Everyone stop!" The others stopped and looked at her. "Now, I want you all to count to ten," Belle said.

"*T*here's no time," Cogsworth protested.

"There's *always* time to be patient," Belle told him.

So they all counted to ten. Everyone seemed calmer, including Phillipe. "If you're patient, it gives you time to make a good plan," Belle explained.

*T*hen Belle started singing a song, and everyone joined in:

Bread must rise
And cakes must bake.
Things must take
The time they take!

So count to ten
And when you're through,
What you've awaited
Will be waiting for you!

Soon Phillipe was free. They fed him hay
and gave him lots of water. Then everyone went
inside. Mrs. Potts served warm gingersnaps.
They all munched happily.

"Now, weren't those worth waiting for?"
Mrs. Potts asked Chip.

"Oh yes, Mama," said Chip cheerfully,
with his mouth full.

"They were indeed,"
agreed Belle.

*L*ater, Belle sank back down into the comfortable cushions in the library. She opened her book and began to read.

*T*hen she reached for a gingersnap and smiled. "Having to wait for something makes it even better when it finally happens," she decided.

The End